AT

Clifford's First Sleepover

For Koto Coltrane Bridwell and her mother, Tsuyu
—N.B.

The author thanks Grace Maccarone and Manny Campana for their contributions to this book.

ISBN 978-0-545-22316-4

10 9 8 7 6 5 4 3 2 1   10 11 12 13 14/0

Printed in the U.S.A.   40

This edition printing, September 2010

SCHOLASTIC READER
LEVEL 1
50-250 WORDS

Clifford's First Sleepover

Norman Bridwell

SCHOLASTIC INC.
New York Toronto London Auckland
Sydney Mexico City New Delhi Hong Kong

Emily Elizabeth is going to
sleep at Grandma's house.

She can take her doll,
but not Clifford.

Emily Elizabeth says good-bye.

She is sad.

She does not see Clifford behind her.

Mom and Dad take Emily Elizabeth
to Grandma's house.

Grandma and Grandpa are
glad to see her.
So is their dog, Lad.

Emily puts her things
in her room at Grandma's.
She still does not see Clifford.

Grandma is cooking dinner.

Yum!

Lad needs a walk before dinner.
Grandma, Grandpa, and Emily
Elizabeth take him outside.

When they leave, Clifford comes out.

Outside, Lad likes to jump.

Inside, Clifford likes to jump, too.

Outside, Lad rolls.

Inside, Clifford rolls, too.

Both dogs like to carry things.

Outside, Lad sees a treat.

Inside, Clifford sees a treat.

Both dogs eat their treats.

Lad likes to run.

Clifford does, too.

Oh, no!

It is time to go home.
Everyone is hungry.

They open the door.

What happened?

They see a big mess
and tiny footprints.

Emily Elizabeth knows who
made the footprints.
And she knows
who made the mess.

Emily Elizabeth finds her puppy.
“How did you get here?” she says.

She helps clean up.

Emily Elizabeth cleans her puppy, too.

Then, Grandpa, Grandma, and
Emily Elizabeth have dinner.

At bedtime, Grandma
makes a bed for Clifford.

Clifford has a better idea.

In the morning,
Emily Elizabeth says good-bye
to her grandparents.
No one will forget
Clifford's first sleepover!